My Sister is an Alien

by RACHEL BRIGHT

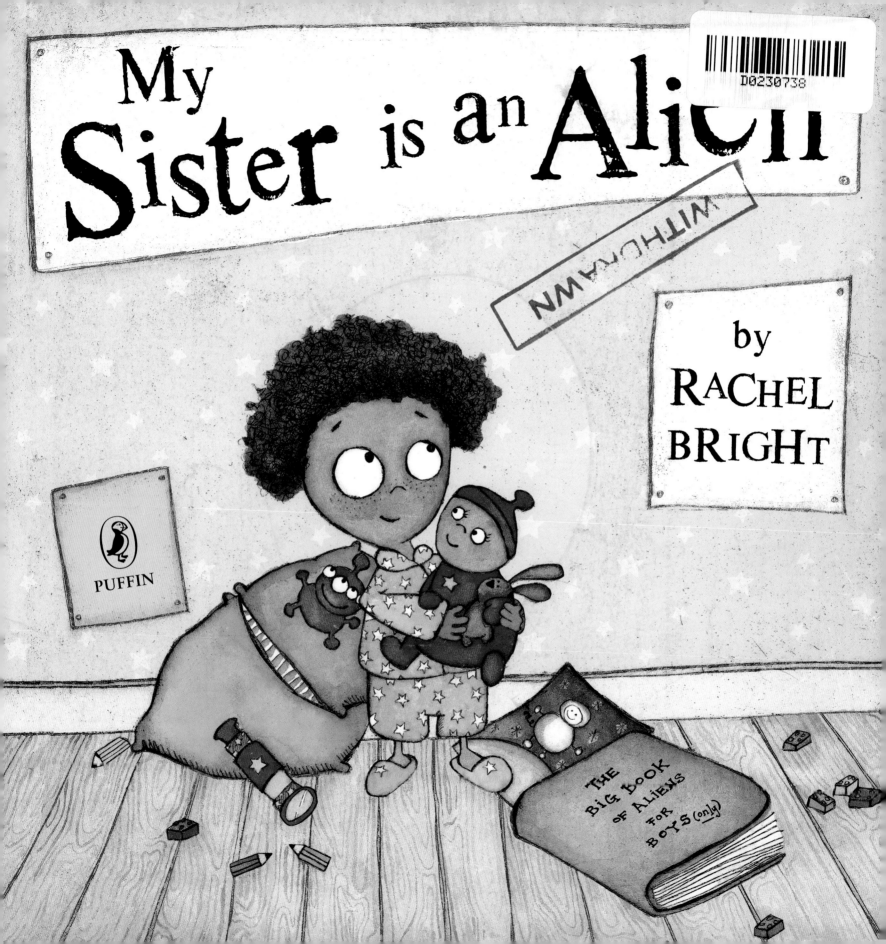

WITHDRAWN

PUFFIN

THE BiG BooK OF ALIEИS FOR BOYS (only)

This is Alfie.

His favourite things are:

1. Aliens
2. Rockets
3. The Moon

In that exact order.

He lives in
a house with
one mummy,

one daddy

and a brand-new sister,
called Ruby.

Mummy talked a lot about Ruby. "Oh, Alfie, isn't she

lovely! Mummy and Daddy are over the moOn!",

But Alfie was thinking about aliens and all he heard was . . .

Daddy talked
a lot about
Ruby too.
"Oh, Alfie, isn't she lovely!
We must make some
Space for her."

MAN TOOLS
AND DAD STUFF.

But Alfie was busy drawing
an astronaut and all
he heard was ...

She looked
like an alien...

She sounded
like an alien...

Goo Goo Goo
Goo Goo Goo
Goo Goo
Goo
Goo Goo
Goo

She **definitely** smelt
like an alien...

...and she often cried for home.

So Alfie decided he must get
Ruby back to the moon,
where she belonged.

And he had
just the thing to
get her there...

...his rocket!

Alfie spent a long time making it nice so Ruby would have a lovely journey home.

He found some space snacks in case Ruby was hungry on the way.

There was just enough time to dress in their spacesuits.

Then at last they were ready to go.

To the Aliens x

Alfie climbed into the rocket
with Ruby (well, somebody responsible
needed to drive) and he began
the countdown . . .

Alfie + Ruby Moon Adventures

mummy and
daddy, we've
gone to the moon,
be back soon.
Love Alfie x
x Ruby x
x

Three . . .

Two . . .

One . . .

LIFT

Alfie and Ruby soared over the treetops and They flew and flew

OFF!

through the air,
into the starry darkness,
towards the moon.

And after not too long, they made a very soft landing.
The moOn was an amazing place!

Ruby looked very happy and the aliens were even more friendly than Alfie thought they would be.

WelcoMe Alfie and Ruby!

They played and played all night long
until Alfie got sleepy and said,
"Ruby, I'd better go home now..."

But when he climbed into the rocket,
he suddenly felt very sad.

"**GOO!**"

Back across the

over the treetops. and

So away they flew,
starry darkness,
all the way home.

That night Ruby slept in Alfie's bed.
"Night, night, Ruby," whispered Alfie
as they snuggled up together.

And Ruby gurgled...
"Goo!"

Now Alfie's
favourite things are:

1. Ruby
2. Aliens
3. Rockets
4. The Moon

In
THAT
exact order.

For my amazing brother and sister
who are, quite simply, out of this world

With super special thanks to Mandy and Goldy
whose magic I couldn't have been without

PUFFIN BOOKS
Published by the Penguin Group: London, New York, Australia,
Canada, India, Ireland, New Zealand and South Africa
Penguin Books Ltd, Registered Offices:
80 Strand, London WC2R 0RL, England

puffinbooks.com

First published 2010
1 3 5 7 9 10 8 6 4 2
Text and illustrations copyright © Rachel Bright, 2010
All rights reserved
The moral right of the author/illustrator has been asserted
Made and printed in China
ISBN: 978–0–141–50265–6